Thumbelina

HANS CHRISTIAN ANDERSEN

TRANSLATED BY R. P. KEIGWIN

Illustrated by

ADRIENNE ADAMS

New York

CHARLES SCRIBNER'S SONS

Thumbelina

Illustrations copyright © 1961 *Adrienne Adams*

The translation by R. P. Keigwin is used by
permission of Flensted Publishers,
Odense, Denmark

This book published simultaneously in the
United States of America and in Canada—
Copyright under the Berne Convention

13 15 17 19 RD/C 20 18 16 14 12
ISBN 684-12705-9 (cloth)

PRINTED IN THE UNITED STATES OF AMERICA

LIBRARY OF CONGRESS CATALOG CARD NUMBER: 61-17282

FOR SUE MANLEY

There was once a woman who did so want to have a wee child of her own, but she had no idea where she was to get it from. So she went off to an old witch and said to her, "I would so dearly like to have a little child. Do please tell me where I can find one."

"Oh, that!" said the witch. "Nothing easier. Take this barleycorn—mind you, it's not the kind that grows out in the fields or that the fowls are fed with. Put it in a flower-pot, and see what happens!"

"Thank you very much," said the woman, giving the witch a shilling. She went straight home and planted the barleycorn, and in no time there came up a lovely great flower which looked just like a tulip, only the petals were shut tight as though it were still in bud.

"It *is* a pretty flower," said the woman, and she gave the lovely red and yellow petals a kiss; but directly she kissed it, the flower burst open with a pop. It was a real tulip—that was plain enough now—but, sitting on the green pistil in the middle of the flower, was a tiny little girl. She was delicately pretty and no taller than your thumb, so she was given the name of Thumbelina.

A nicely varnished walnut-shell did for her cradle, blue violet petals for her mattress, and a rose-leaf for her counterpane. That was where she slept at night; but in the daytime she played about on the table, where the woman had put a plate with a wreath of flowers. These dipped their stalks

down into the water, in the middle of which floated a large tulip petal where Thumbelina could sit and row herself from one side of the plate to the other, using a couple of white horsehairs as oars. It was a most charming sight. She could sing, too, in the sweetest little voice you ever heard.

One night, as she lay in her pretty bed, a hideous toad came hopping in through a broken pane in the window. It was a great ugly slimy toad, and it jumped straight down on to the table where Thumbelina was lying asleep under her red rose-leaf.

"She would make a nice wife for my son," thought the toad, and she snatched up the walnut-shell in which Thumbelina was sleeping and hopped off with her through the window into the garden.

There was a wide brook running through it, but the bank was swampy and muddy, and here the toad lived with her son. Ugh! Wasn't he ugly and horrible—just like his mother! "Koax, koax, brekke-ke-kex!" was all he could say, when he saw the pretty little girl in the walnut-shell.

"Sh! Not so loud, or you'll wake her," said the old toad. "She might yet run away from us, for she's as light as swan's-down. Let's put her out in the brook on one of those broad water lilies. She's so small and light that its leaf will be like an island for her. She can't escape from there, and in the meantime we'll get the best room ready under the mud for you two to live in."

There were quite a lot of water lilies growing on the water with their broad green leaves which seem to be floating on the surface. The biggest of them all happened to be the farthest away, but the old toad swam out and placed the walnut-shell on it with Thumbelina still sleeping inside.

Early the next morning the poor little thing woke up and, when she saw where she was, she began to cry bitterly, for the big green leaf had water all 'round it and she couldn't possibly reach the bank.

The old toad stayed down in the mud and decorated her room with rushes and yellow water lilies, so as to make everything quite snug for her new daughter-in-law. Then she swam out with her son to the water lily where Thumbelina was standing, for they wanted to fetch that fine walnut bed and put it up in the bridal-chamber before she came herself. The old toad made a low curtsey to her in the water and said, "Here's my son— he's to be your husband. You'll have a lovely home together down in the mud."

"Koax, koax, brekke-ke-kex!" was all that the son could say.

Then they took the pretty little bed and swam away with it. But Thumbelina sat all alone on the green leaf and cried, for she didn't want to live with the horrible toad or to marry her ugly son. The little fishes, swimming down there in the water, had caught sight of the toad and heard what she said. So they poked their heads out of the water; they were so anxious to have a look at the little girl. Directly they saw her, they found her charming, and they couldn't bear to think that she must go and live with the ugly toad. No, that must never happen! They all swarmed together down in the water round the green stalk that held the leaf she was standing on and gnawed it through with their teeth; whereupon the leaf floated away with Thumbelina down the brook, far away where the toad could never reach her.

Thumbelina went sailing past all sorts of places, and the little birds perched in the bushes saw her and trilled out, "What a pretty little lady!"

The leaf that carried her floated farther and farther on; and thus it was that Thumbelina began her journey abroad.

A dainty little white butterfly kept on fluttering 'round and 'round her, till at last it settled on the leaf, for it had taken a great liking for Thumbelina; and she too was pleased, because the toad couldn't reach her now and she was sailing through such a lovely part of the brook. The sunshine gleamed on the water like the finest gold. Then she took her

sash and tied one end of it 'round the butterfly, while the other end she made fast to the leaf; and this at once gathered speed—and so did Thumbelina because, you see, she was standing on the leaf.

Just then a large cockchafer came flying up and, catching sight of her, clutched her 'round her slender waist and flew with her up into a tree. But the green leaf went floating on and the butterfly with it, because it had been tied to the leaf and couldn't manage to free itself.

Gracious, what a fright it gave poor Thumbelina, when the cock-chafer flew up into the tree with her! Still, what upset her even more was the thought of the pretty white butterfly that she had tied to the leaf; for unless it could manage to free itself, it would certainly starve to death. But that didn't worry the cockchafer in the slightest. He settled beside her on the largest green leaf in the tree, gave her some nectar from the blossoms and said how pretty she was, although she wasn't a bit like a cockchafer. Later on, all the other cockchafers living in the tree came to call on her. They stared at Thumbelina, and the young lady cock-chafers shrugged their feelers—"Why, she's only got two legs," they said. "What a pitiable sight!"

"She hasn't any feelers," they went on. "She's so pinched in at the waist—ugh! She might almost be a human. Isn't she ugly!" exclaimed all the lady cockchafers. And yet Thumbelina was really so pretty. And that's what the cockchafer thought who had carried her off; but when all the others kept saying how ugly she was, then at length he thought so too and would have nothing to do with her; she could go where she liked. They flew with her down from the tree and sat her on a daisy. There she cried and cried, because she was so ugly that the cockchafers wouldn't have her; and all the time she was as beautiful as can be—as exquisite as the loveliest rose-petal.

Right through the summer poor Thumbelina lived quite alone in that enormous wood. She took blades of grass and plaited herself a bed, which

she hung under a large dock-leaf, so as to be out of the rain. She got her food from the honey in the flowers, and her drink from the morning dew on the leaves; and in this way summer and autumn went by.

But now came winter—the long, cold winter. All the birds that had sung to her so beautifully now flew away; the trees and flowers withered; the great dock-leaf she had been living under furled itself into nothing but a faded yellow stalk. She felt the cold most terribly, for her clothes were by this time in tatters, and she herself was so tiny and delicate, poor Thumbelina, that she would surely be frozen to death. It began snowing, and every snowflake that fell on her was like a whole shovel-ful being thrown on us, for we are quite big and she was no taller than your thumb. So she wrapped herself up in a dead leaf, but there was no warmth in that, and she shivered with cold.

On the fringe of the wood where she had now come to was a large cornfield; but the corn had long been harvested, and only the bare barren stubble thrust up from the frozen earth. It was just like an entire forest for her to walk through—oh, and she was shivering with cold!

At length she came to the field-mouse's door. It was a little hole down below the stubble. There the field-mouse had a fine snug place to live in, with a whole roomful of corn and a splendid kitchen and dining-room.

Poor Thumbelina stood just inside the door like any other wretched beggar-girl and asked for a little bit of barleycorn, for she hadn't had a scrap to eat for two days.

"You poor mite!" said the field-mouse, for at heart she was a kind old thing. "Come you in and have a bite with me in my warm room."

As she at once took a liking to Thumbelina she made a suggestion. "You're quite welcome to stay with me for the winter," she said, "as long as you'll keep my rooms nice and tidy and also tell me stories, for I'm so fond of stories." And Thumbelina did what the kind old field-mouse asked for and was extremely comfortable there.

"I dare say we shall have a visitor before long," said the field-mouse. "My neighbor generally pays me a call once a week. His house is even snugger than mine, with good-sized rooms, and he wears such a lovely black velvet coat. If only you could get him for a husband, you'd be comfortably off. But his sight's very bad. You must tell him all the nicest stories you know."

Thumbelina took no notice of all this; she had no intention of marrying the neighbor, for he was a mole. He came and called in his black velvet coat. He was so rich and clever, according to the field-mouse, and his home was twenty times the size of the field-mouse's. He was very learned, but he couldn't bear sunshine and pretty flowers; he said all sorts of nasty things about them, never having seen them. Thumbelina had to sing, and she sang both "Ladybird, ladybird, fly away home" and "Ring-a-ring-o'roses;" and the mole fell in love with her because of her pretty voice, but he didn't say anything—he was much too cautious a man for that.

He had lately dug a long passage for himself through the earth, leading from his house to theirs. Here the field-mouse and Thumbelina were invited to stroll whenever they cared to. But he told them not to be afraid of the dead bird lying in the passage; it was a whole bird with beak and feathers, that had evidently only just died as the winter began and was now buried in the very spot where he made his underground passage.

The mole took a bit of touchwood in his mouth—for in the dark that shines just like fire—and went ahead to give them a light in the long dark passage. When they came to where the dead bird was lying, the mole

tilted his broad snout up to the ceiling and thrust through the earth; making a large hole through which the light could penetrate.

In the middle of the floor lay a dead swallow with its pretty wings folded close in to its sides, and head and legs tucked in beneath its feathers. The poor bird must have died of cold. Thumbelina felt so sorry for it; she was very fond of all the little birds that had sung and twittered for her so sweetly right through the summer. But the mole kicked at it with his stumpy legs, saying, "That won't chirp any more! How wretched it must be to be born a little bird! Thank goodness no child of

mine will ever be. A bird like that has of course nothing but its twitter and is bound to starve to death when winter comes.''

"Just what I'd expect to hear from a sensible man like you," said the field-mouse. "What has a bird to show for all its twittering, when winter comes? It must starve and freeze. But I suppose that's considered a great thing.''

Thumbelina didn't say a word, but when the other two turned their backs on the bird, she stooped down and, smoothing aside the feathers that lay over its head, she kissed its closed eyes. "Who knows—this may be the very one," she thought, "that used to sing so beautifully to me last summer.''

The mole now filled in the hole where the daylight shone through and saw the two ladies home. But that night Thumbelina simply couldn't sleep; so she got up and plaited a fine big blanket of hay, which she carried down and spread all over the dead bird, and she took some soft cotton-wool she had found in the field-mouse's room and tucked this in at the sides, so that the bird might lie warm in the cold earth.

"Goodbye, you lovely little bird," she said. "Goodbye, and thank you for your beautiful singing last summer, when all the trees were green and the sun was so bright and warm.'' Then she laid her head up against the bird's breast—but at the same moment she got such a fright, for she heard a kind of thumping inside. It was the bird's heart. The bird wasn't dead; it had been lying numb and unconscious and now, as it grew warm again, it revived.

You see, in autumn the swallows all fly away to the warm countries, but if there's one that lags behind it gets so cold that it falls down dead. There it lies, where it fell, and the cold snow covers it over.

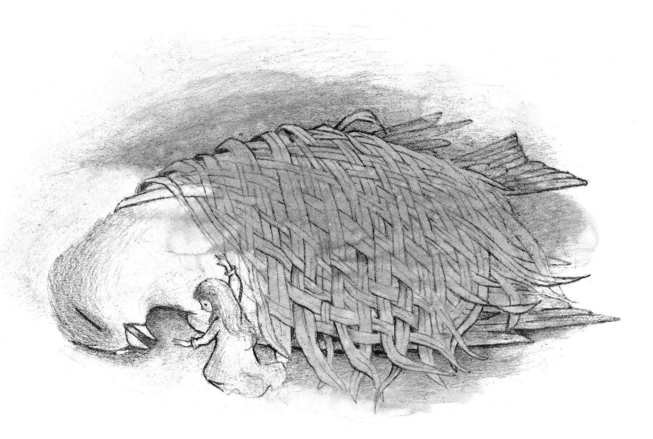

Thumbelina was all of a tremble from the fright she had, for the bird was of course an immense great creature beside her, who was no taller than your thumb. However, she took courage and tucked the cotton-wool still more closely round the poor swallow and fetched a curled mint leaf that she had been using herself for a counterpane and spread this over the bird's head.

The following night she again stole down to the bird, and this time it had quite revived; but it was so feeble that it could only open its eyes for a short moment to look at Thumbelina, standing there with a bit of touch-wood in her hand, for she had no other light.

"Thank you, my darling child," said the sick swallow. "I'm lovely and warm now. I shall soon get back my strength and be able to fly again, out in the warm sunshine."

"Ah, but it's so cold out of doors," she said. "It's snowing and freezing. Stay in your warm bed; I'll look after you all right."

Then she brought the swallow some water, in the petal of a flower, and the bird drank it and told her how it had torn one of its wings on a bramble and therefore couldn't fly as fast as the other swallows when they flew far, far away to the warm countries. At last it had fallen to the ground, but it couldn't remember anything after that and had no idea how it came to be where it was.

The swallow now remained here all through the winter, and Thumbelina took care of it and grew very fond of it. Neither the mole nor the

field-mouse heard anything at all about this; they had no liking for the poor wretched swallow.

As soon as spring had arrived and the sun had begun to warm the earth, the swallow said goodbye to Thumbelina, who opened up the hole that the mole had made in the roof of the passage. The sun came shining in so pleasantly, and the swallow asked if she would like to come too; she could sit on its back, and they would fly far out into the green forest. But Thumbelina knew that it would grieve the old field-mouse, if she left her like that.

"No, I can't," said Thumbelina. "Goodbye, goodbye, you dear kind girl," said the swallow, as it flew in-to the open sunshine. Thumbelina gazed after it with tears in her eyes, for she was so fond of the poor swallow.

"Tweet-tweet!" sang the bird and flew off into the woods . . . .

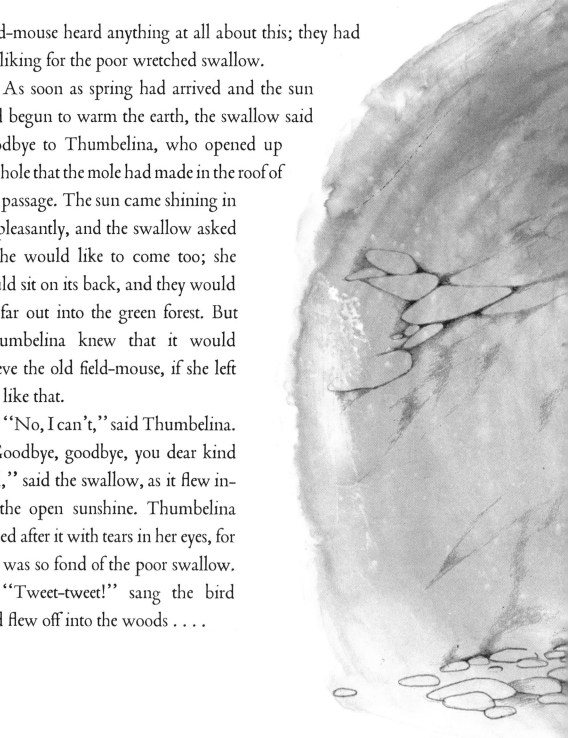

Thumbelina felt so sad. She was never allowed to go out into the warm sunshine. The corn that had been sown in the field above the field-mouse's home was certainly very tall; so that it was like a dense wood for the poor little girl, who after all was only an inch high.

"You will have to start making your wedding trousseau this summer," the field-mouse told her, because by now their neighbor, the tiresome tedious mole in the black velvet coat, had proposed to her. "You'll need to have both woolens and linen—something for every occasion—when you're married to the mole."

So Thumbelina had to spin from a distaff, and the field-mouse engaged four spiders to spin and weave day and night. Every evening there was a visit from the mole, who always kept on about how, when summer

was over, the sun wasn't nearly so warm, whereas now it scorched the earth till it was as hard as a stone. Yes, and when the summer had ended there was to be his wedding with Thumbelina. But she wasn't at all pleased, for she found the mole such a terrible bore.

Every morning, as the sun rose, and every evening as it set, she stole out to the door, and when the wind parted the ears of corn so that she could see the blue sky, she thought how lovely and bright it was out there and did so wish she could catch sight of the dear swallow once more; but the bird never came again and had evidently flown far off into the beautiful green forest.

Now it was autumn, and Thumbelina had the whole of her trousseau ready.

"Your wedding will be in four weeks' time," the field-mouse told her. But Thumbelina wept and said she wouldn't marry the tedious mole.

"Hoity-toity!" said the field-mouse. "Don't you be so pig-headed, or I'll bite you with my white teeth. Why, he's a splendid husband for you. The Queen herself hasn't anything like his black velvet coat. His kitchen and cellar are both of the best. You ought to thank Heaven he's yours."

The wedding day arrived. The mole was already there to fetch Thumbelina. She would have to live with him deep down under the earth and never come out into the warm sunshine, for he didn't care for that.

The poor child was very sad at having to say goodbye to the beautiful sun, which she had at least been allowed to look at from the doorway when she was living with the field-mouse.

"Goodbye, bright sun!" she said and, stretching out her arms to it, she also took a few steps out from the field-mouse's dwelling; for the harvest was in, and nothing was left but the dry stubble. "Goodbye, goodbye," she said, throwing her tiny arms 'round a little red flower standing near. "Remember me to the dear swallow, if you happen to see it."

"Tweet-tweet!" she heard suddenly over her head. She looked up, and there was the swallow just passing. How delighted it was to see Thumbelina.

She told the bird how she disliked having to marry the ugly mole and to live deep down under the earth where the sun never shone. She couldn't help crying at the thought.

"The cold winter will soon be here," said the swallow. "I'm going far away to the warm countries. Will you come with me? You can sit on my back. Just tie yourself on with your sash, and away we'll fly from the ugly mole and his dingy house, far away across the mountains, to the

warm countries, where the sun shines more brightly than it does here and there's always summer with its lovely flowers. Dear little Thumbelina, do come with me—you who saved my life when I lay frozen stiff in that dismal cellar.''

"Yes, I'll come with you," said Thumbelina. She climbed on to the bird's back, setting her feet on its outstretched wings and tieing her sash to one of the strongest feathers.

Then the swallow flew high up into the air, over lake and forest, high up over the great mountains of eternal snow. Thumbelina shivered in the cold air, but then she snuggled in under the bird's warm feathers, merely poking out her little head to look at all the loveliness stretched out beneath her.

And at last they reached the warm countries. The sun was shining there much more brightly than with us, and the sky looked twice as far off. On walls and slopes grew the finest black and white grapes, in the woods hung lemons and oranges; the air smelt sweetly of myrtle and curled mint, and the most delightful children darted about on the roads playing with large gay-colored butterflies.

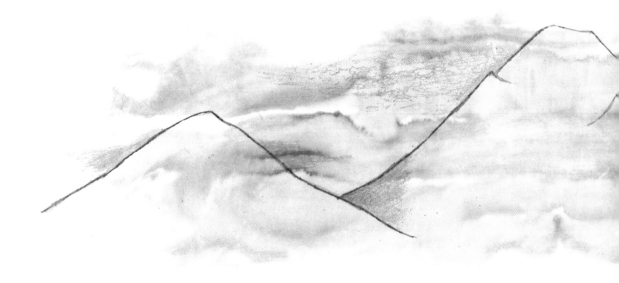

But the swallow kept flying on and on, and the country became more and more beautiful, till at last they came upon an ancient palace of glittering white marble standing among vivid green trees beside a blue lake. Vines went curling up 'round the tall pillars, and right at the top were a number of swallows' nests. One of these was the home of the swallow that had brought Thumbelina on its back.

"Here's my house," cried the swallow. "But you see those beautiful flowers growing down there? You shall now choose one of them yourself, and then I'll put you on it, and you can make yourself as cosy as you like."

"That will be lovely," she said, clapping her little hands.

A large white marble column was lying there on the ground just as it had fallen and broken into three pieces, but in among these were growing the most beautiful white flowers. The swallow flew down with Thumbelina and placed her on one of the broad petals—but what a surprise

she got! There in the middle of the flower sat a little man as white and transparent as if he had been made of glass. He wore the neatest little gold crown on his head and the most exquisite wings on his shoulders; he himself was no bigger than Thumbelina. He was the guardian spirit of the flower. Each flower had just such a little man or woman living in it, but this one was King of them all.

"Goodness, how handsome he is!" whispered Thumbelina to the swallow. The little monarch was very frightened of the swallow, which of course seemed a gigantic bird beside one so small and delicate as himself; but when he caught sight of Thumbelina he was enchanted, for she was much the prettiest little lady he had ever seen. So he took the gold crown off his head and placed it on hers. At the same time he asked her what her name was and whether she would be his wife; if so, she would become Queen of all the flowers. Well, he would be a proper husband

for her, quite different from the son of the old toad and from the mole with the black velvet coat. So she said yes to the handsome King, and from every flower there appeared a lady or a gentleman that was the most dapper little creature imaginable. Each one brought a present for Thumbelina, but the best of them all was a pair of beautiful wings from a large white fly. These were fastened to her back, so that she too could flit from flower to flower. There was such rejoicing, and the swallow sat up above in its nest and sang for them as well as it could, but the poor bird was really too sad at heart, for it was very fond of Thumbelina and would have liked never to be parted from her.

"You shan't be called Thumbelina," said the guardian spirit of the flower to her. "It's an ugly name, and you are so pretty. We will call you Maia."

"Goodbye, goodbye," said the swallow and flew away again from the warm countries, far away back to Denmark. There it had a little nest above the window where the man lives who can tell fairy tales, and there it was that the swallow sang "tweet-tweet!" to him. . . . And that's where the whole story comes from.